THE DOODLES OF SAM DIBBLE

OF SAM DIBBLE

Robots Don't Clean Toilets

THE DOODLES OF SAM DIBBLE

Robots Don't Clean Toilets

by J. Press

illustrated by Michael Kline

Grosset & Dunlap
An Imprint of Penguin Group (USA) Inc.

GROSSET & DUNLAP
Published by the Penguin Group
Penguin Group (USA) Inc., 375 Hudson Street, New York, New York 10014, USA
Penguin Group (Canada), 90 Eglinton Avenue East, Suite 700, Toronto,
Ontario M4P 2Y3, Canada (a division of Pearson Penguin Canada Inc.)
Penguin Books Ltd, 80 Strand, London WC2R 0RL, England
Penguin Ireland, 25 St Stephen's Green, Dublin 2, Ireland (a division of Penguin Books Ltd)
Penguin Group (Australia), 707 Collins Street, Melbourne, Victoria 3008, Australia
(a division of Pearson Australia Group Pty Ltd)
Penguin Books India Pvt Ltd, 11 Community Centre, Panchsheel Park,
New Delhi—110 017, India
Penguin Group (NZ), 67 Apollo Drive, Rosedale, Auckland 0632, New Zealand
(a division of Pearson New Zealand Ltd)
Penguin Books (South Africa), Rosebank Office Park, 181 Jan Smuts Avenue,
Parktown North 2193, South Africa
Penguin China, B7 Jiaming Center, 27 East Third Ring Road North,
Chaoyang District, Beijing 100020, China

Penguin Books Ltd, Registered Offices: 80 Strand, London WC2R 0RL, England

Designed by Debbie Guy-Christiansen

Text copyright © 2013 by Judy Press. Illustrations copyright © 2013 by
Michael Kline. All rights reserved. Published by Grosset & Dunlap, a division of Penguin
Young Readers Group, 345 Hudson Street, New York, New York 10014. GROSSET &
DUNLAP is a trademark of Penguin Group (USA) Inc. Printed in the U.S.A.

Library of Congress Cataloging-in-Publication Data is available.

ISBN 978-0-448-46109-0   10 9 8 7 6 5 4 3 2 1

ALWAYS LEARNING   **PEARSON**

For Allan, the world's greatest Pepe—JP

To Tina Fey: Just look at what you've done—MK

Chapter One
A Bottle Rocket Doodle

My name is Sam Dibble. I can bounce a

basketball between my legs, spit watermelon

seeds across a room, and balance a spoon on

my nose. But what I like to do most is doodle.

1

I think doodling is a lot of fun. It's like taking your pen for a walk and going someplace you've never been before.

My grandpa Dibble says all Dibbles doodle.

"Why, even your third cousin twice removed Picasso Dibble doodled."

"What happened to him?" I asked Grandpa.

"He got in trouble, yes indeed. Drew a doodle of his teacher with two heads," Grandpa told me.

I go to Colfax Elementary School, and my teacher's name is Mrs. Hennessey.

She has radar implanted in her head that beeps when kids are fooling around.

In school we were learning about inventors and their inventions. I was busy doodling my favorite invention on the back of my math workbook.

Suddenly, Wax Baxter jumped up out of his seat. "Mrs. Hennessey, Sam's doodling!" he shouted.

Wax is the biggest tattletale in third grade. His real name is Max, but everyone calls him "Wax" because one time we had a contest to see who could pick the most wax from our ears and he won.

And here's the thing that stinks worse

than the cheese sandwich I left in my backpack

over summer vacation: Wax's dad is my mom's

boyfriend!

Mrs. H. told Wax to sit down and me to

pay attention.

"Class, who can name an important

invention?" Mrs. H. asked.

Meghan Diaz called out, "The computer! Because I can play games on it. And learn things."

Nicole McDonald said, "The car. It's too far to walk to the mall."

"Anyone else?" Mrs. H. asked.

My friend Cookie raised his hand. "TV!" he shouted. "So I can watch sports and my favorite shows."

Cookie's real name is Reginald Cook. He's my second-best friend, and he can name every pro basketball player.

No one gets too close to Cookie, because he farts.

STAY BACK 50 FEET!

Then Robert Chen raised his hand. "I think

the wheel is an important invention. Without it

we wouldn't have cars or computers or lots of

other things."

Robert's my best friend. He's really smart,

and he lets me copy off him sometimes.

"Class, next Friday, we are having our annual Invention Fair! Your invention must be original. If you don't want to make the actual invention, you can make a prototype, which is a working model of your invention. Or you can draw a picture of an invention you'd like to make. But be sure to include a set of instructions that describes how it works."

Meghan raised her hand. "Mrs. Hennessey, can Nicole and I invent something together?" she asked.

"You can work individually or as a team," Mrs. H. answered.

I knew I was picking Robert to be my

partner. Together we'd win first prize at the

Invention Fair!

I looked over at Robert and gave him our

secret signal, but I don't think he saw it.

"Mrs. Hennessey, can my dad help me

make my invention?" Wax asked.

"A grown-up can help you with tools or materials that might be dangerous. But the idea and most of the work should be your own."

Next Nicole said, "What if we don't know what to invent?"

Mrs. H. went up to the whiteboard. "Here are some ideas to get you started," she said.

1. Invent a new toy or game.

2. Invent something to improve safety for an animal or person.

3. Invent something that will make your daily life easier, more productive, or more fun.

Maybe I'll invent a magic eraser and make

Wax Baxter disappear!

Just then, there was a knock on our

classroom door, and Mrs. Lewis, the school

principal, walked in.

Uh-oh! Someone's

getting in trouble, and it

better not be me!

Chapter Two

A Statue of Liberty Doodle

"Good morning, class," Mrs. Lewis said. "I'd like you to give a warm welcome to your new classmate, Bradley Wilson."

Everyone shouted, "Hello, Bradley Wilson!"

The new kid was standing next to Mrs. Lewis, and he looked like he'd rather be somewhere else.

"Bradley moved here from New York City," Mrs. H. explained, pointing to New York State on our classroom map.

My grandpa told me the Statue of Liberty is in New York Harbor. "She got seasick, Sammy-boy. That's why she turned green!"

Mrs. Lewis turned to face Bradley. "I know you'll be very happy in Mrs. Hennessey's class," she said. "Please stop by my office after school and let me know how you're doing."

Uh-oh. He'd better be careful. The fifth

graders said one time a kid got sent to Mrs.

Lewis's office and they never saw him again!

My mom said I shouldn't believe everything

the big kids say, because they're just trying to

scare us. But the new kid shouldn't go there,

anyway!

After Mrs. Lewis left the classroom, Mrs.

H. told the new kid he could sit at the empty

desk next to Robert. That used to be my

desk, but Mrs. H. said I had to move.

Mrs. H. said he could ask Robert for help.

Then she told Bradley that the Invention

Fair was next week. "Why don't you work with

Robert? He can tell you more about it," she

said.

I couldn't believe my ears. "But Mrs. H.!" I

started to say.

"Yes, Sam?" Mrs. H. asked.

Robert looked back at me, but there wasn't enough time for our secret signal.

"Robert was going to work with me!"

"You and Robert have worked on a lot of projects together. Sometimes it's good to work with new people."

I didn't want to work with new people. But Mrs. H. was already telling the class we had to give an oral report about an inventor on Monday.

Here's why I didn't want to stand up in front of the whole class:

1. What if I had a booger hanging out of my nose?

2. What if I got a

hole in my pants

and everyone

could see my

underwear?

3. What if I forgot what I was going to

say and nothing came out?

The new kid raised his hand.

"Yes, Bradley?" Mrs. H. said.

"In my old school we acted like the person when we gave our reports."

"That's a very good idea," Mrs. H. said. "And it sounds like fun."

What's fun about standing up in front of the whole class dressed as Ben Franklin wearing short pants and little round glasses?

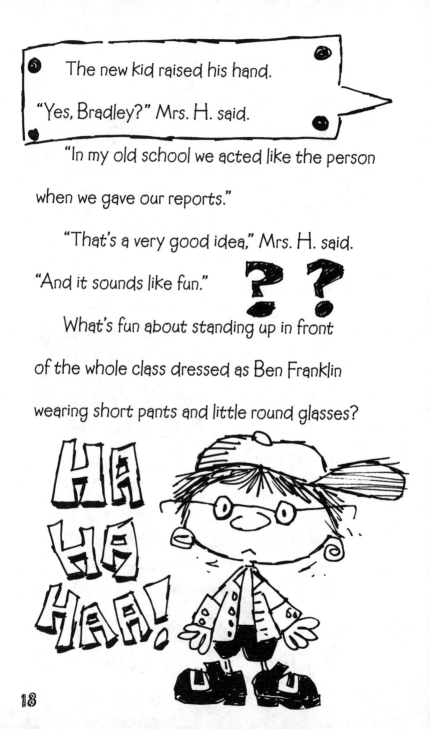

Thanks to New Kid, I'll now look like the biggest dork ever!

It was time for silent reading. "Please choose a book about inventors from the shelf," Mrs. H. said.

I walked over to the bookshelf and got a book about Benjamin Franklin. He invented the lightning rod when he flew a kite in a storm.

On my way back to my desk, I heard New Kid talking to Robert. And he didn't even get into trouble!

"Who're you doing your report on?" he asked Robert. "I'm doing mine on Dr. Jonas Salk."

I smiled to myself. That doctor dude sounded boring. I mean, what could a doctor have invented that is so great?

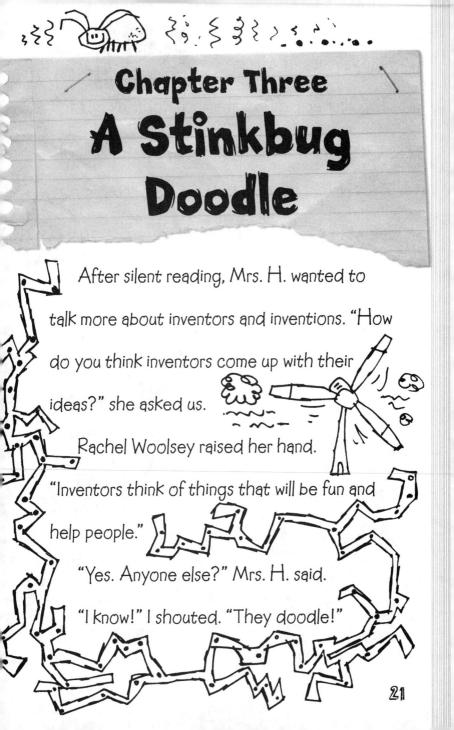

Chapter Three
A Stinkbug Doodle

After silent reading, Mrs. H. wanted to talk more about inventors and inventions. "How do you think inventors come up with their ideas?" she asked us.

Rachel Woolsey raised her hand.

"Inventors think of things that will be fun and help people."

"Yes. Anyone else?" Mrs. H. said.

"I know!" I shouted. "They doodle!"

Wax let out a laugh.

"Rachel and Sam are both right," Mrs. H. said. "Inventors draw pictures of their inventions. They also observe friends, families, and pets to see what problem they can solve."

I grabbed my pen and wrote down a list of my family's problems:

My mom:

⚠ 1. She likes Wax's dad

⚠ 2. She sings out of tune

⚠ 3. She talks loud when she's angry

Grandpa Dibble:

1. My mom says he tells too many stories
2. He snores really loud
3. His teeth come out at night

My cat Fang:

1. Her litter box stinks
2. She sleeps all day
3. She has sharp claws

My problems:

1. My mom likes Wax's dad
2. I can't find my stinkbug
3. Homework

MISSING

When the lunch bell rang, I folded up my list and stuck it in my backpack. Then I headed down to the lunchroom.

Everyone in school was talking about the Invention Fair. They couldn't wait for it to start.

I got in the lunch line and grabbed a carton of milk. Then I carried my tray over to a table and sat down next to Robert and New Kid.

"Bradley has a motorcycle," Robert said. "And he's letting me ride it."

"It's no big deal," New Kid said. "It's only a Turbine Superbike. I'm getting a V10 Superbike next. It costs more money, but my dad said he'll buy it for me."

"My grandpa drives a cool car," I said. "He told me it's worth lots of money. Like a hundred bucks."

"A hundred bucks? You're really funny, Walter," New Kid said, laughing.

I was about to tell New Kid that he got my name wrong when Wax sat down next to us.

"Brad, I just remembered I have to go to the orthodontist this afternoon," he said. "So I can't come over to your house with Robert."

I turned to Robert. "Hey, what's going on?"

"Bradley invited us over to play basketball," Robert said. "He has a hoop in his backyard."

"Even Wax?"

New Kid slapped Wax on the back. "Yeah, Wax is cool.

"You can come, too, I guess," New Kid said.

"Since Wax can't make it."

"Yeah," said Robert.

"Nah," I said, "I gotta go home and find my stinkbug."

After lunch, our class went outside to the yard. A bunch of girls were hanging around by the swings.

"Hi, Rachel!" I called out. Rachel is the most popular girl in third grade, and the class president. She likes girly things, but she's okay because she picked me to be class vice president. **VP!**

"Hi, Sam," Rachel said, but she was looking at New Kid. Then she sang out, "Hi, Brad-leeee," and all the girls started giggling.

"Hey, let's play some b-ball," New Kid said. "At my old school, I was captain of our basketball team and we won the championship game."

"Brad's on my team," Wax said quickly, as we hurried over to the court.

"Sure," said New Kid. "You, me, and Robert can be one team."

"But . . ." I started.

"What's the big deal, Dribble?" Wax asked.

"Nothing." I asked Cookie to be on my team. "We can play three on three. It's you and me against Wax, Robert, and New Kid. We just need one more player."

29

I looked around and spotted Marvin Willis, the oldest kid in third grade. He has a mustache and real muscles, not like the kind you get from stuffing your T-shirt with socks.

With Marvin on our team, there was no way we'd lose the game!

Chapter Four
A Toilet Bowl Doodle

Mr. Howell was the teacher on yard duty. Everyone calls him "Mr. Owl" because he looks like the stuffed owl that's in his classroom.

"Each hoop you make is one point," Mr. Owl said, handing the ball to Wax. "And seven points wins the game."

Mr. Owl blew his whistle to start the game.

Marvin stood in front of Wax to block his shot.

"Hey, that's not fair!" Wax complained. "You

brought in Marvin just so you could win."

 Wax crouched down low and tried to get

by Marvin, but he lost the ball. Marvin scooped

it up and passed the ball to me.

 I caught the ball with one hand and

bounced it off the backboard for a quick layup.

"Yay, that's one point for us!" I shouted.

New Kid picked up the ball and dribbled it to Robert, who tossed it into the hoop and made a basket.

Tie game

"Yeah!" Robert shouted. "Game's tied, one to one."

We got the ball back, and Cookie tried for a layup. The ball swooshed through the basket and we scored another point.

Next Wax dribbled the ball past Cookie and passed it to New Kid. He scored and we were tied again.

I grabbed the ball and tossed it toward the basket. The ball bounced off the backboard and hit New Kid in the face!

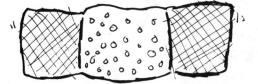

"Oops, sorry," I said.

But New Kid wasn't listening. "Call a plastic surgeon!" he shouted, holding his hand over his nose.

"Move aside," Mr. Owl said, making his way onto the court. "We've got a player down."

"You did that on purpose, Dribble!" Wax yelled.

"I didn't, Wax! It was an accident. And I said I was sorry."

Mr. Owl helped New Kid up off the ground. "He's fine," he declared. "Get back to your game, kids. Recess is almost over."

We finished playing the game, and I scored the winning point. New Kid said his team would've won if he hadn't gotten injured.

When we got back to class, Mrs. H. said we had to research the inventor we picked for our oral report.

I didn't want to do my report on Ben Franklin, so I used the computer to look up who invented basketball. I found out it was a

man called James Naismith. I asked Mrs. H. if I

could use him instead of Benjamin Franklin.

Peach basket

Basketball is a very important invention.

When I get older, I want to play in the pros and

make millions of dollars.

Mrs. H. said I could switch if no one else was doing a report on him.

I walked back to the computers. "Hey, is anyone doing James Naismith?" I asked.

"Who's that?" asked Cookie.

"He invented basketball."

"I'm doing my report on him!" New Kid said.

"What? No, you weren't. You just stole my idea!"

"But you picked Ben Franklin," New Kid insisted.

"Well, I don't want to dress up like him, so I switched."

New Kid shrugged. "Too bad. I picked

James Naismith before you did."

Great. Now I had to pick some other

inventor. I thought for a few minutes and then

had a good idea.

I did a search for

the words *toilet bowl*

and *inventor.*

The name Thomas Crapper popped up on

the computer screen.

Chapter Five

A Belly-Button-
Lint Picker Doodle

The last bell rang, and Mrs. H. told us to pack up our things and get ready to go home. I knew Robert couldn't walk home with me since he was going to New Kid's house. But I tried to convince him not to go.

"You don't even know him," I told Robert. "What if his house is haunted and vampires live there?"

"I don't care," Robert told me. "Besides, he said I could ride on his motorbike!"

If Robert went over there, he and New Kid would be best friends and do everything together!

"Why can't Wax be his partner? Then we could work together."

"I wanted to be your partner, but now I can't. There's always next year!" Robert said. Then he put on his jacket and waved good-bye.

Cookie lives next door to me, so we walked home together. "Do you want to play video games?"

"I can't," I told him. "I'm working on my invention. It's going to be a robot that will do my chores, like cleaning the toilet."

"Wow! You must be a superbrain to come up with something like that."

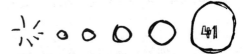

When I got home, Grandpa was watching

TV. I plopped down on the couch next to him.

"How'd your day go, Sammy-boy?"

Grandpa asked.

"Bad. Robert's working with some new kid

on his invention for the Invention Fair. And now

I have no one to help me make my robot."

"I can give you a hand," Grandpa offered, turning off the TV. "Got my tools in the garage."

Then my mom came into the living room. She was carrying a tray of cookies and two glasses of milk. "Sam, I thought you and Lucy would like a snack," she said.

"Why is Lucy coming here?" I shouted.

Lucy is Wax's annoying little sister. She has pigtails that stick out from the sides of her head and is missing her two front teeth.

"Mr. Baxter is taking Max to the orthodontist, and I offered to keep an eye on her," my mom said.

The doorbell rang and my mom went to get it. I looked out the living room window and saw Wax waiting in the car.

VRRMMM RRMM..

Wax's dad owns a funeral home, and he touches dead bodies every day. When Mr.

Baxter sees me, he wants to shake my hand. But I tell him I can't because I just picked my nose.

Mr. Baxter and Lucy walked into the living room. "Guess what, Sammy Bibble-Dribble? I lost another tooth," Lucy said.

"I don't care. I've got something important to do, so don't get in my way."

"Okeydokey," Lucy said. Then she stuck her tongue out at me.

Before Mr. Baxter left, he invited us to

dinner at his house next week to meet his

family, and my mom said we would go.

At their house with all the dead people?

No way!

I didn't have time to think about eating

dinner at Wax's house. I had to start working

on my robot. Lucy followed Grandpa and me
out to the garage.

"Got some valuable things in here,"
Grandpa said, lifting up the garage door.
"Never know when they'll come in handy."

In the garage were empty paint cans,
rusted tire wheels, strings of Christmas lights,
screws and nails scattered on the ground, and
old cardboard boxes.

"Grandpa, can we make a robot from all this junk?" I said, looking around.

"Use your imagination, Sammy-boy. That's what inventing is all about."

Lucy raced over and picked up a guitar that was missing its strings. "I want this," she said. "I'm going to learn how to play it."

"Don't touch anything," I warned Lucy. "I might need it for my robot."

STOP

"My brother Max told me he's inventing a belly-button-lint picker," Lucy said. "And he's going to win first prize."

1st

"My robot will be better," I told Lucy.

I took another look around at the stuff in Grandpa's garage. I wish Robert were here to help me!

If I can't come up with a robot that cleans toilets, I'll have to clean them myself!

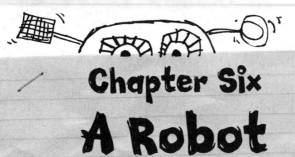

Chapter Six
A Robot Doodle

Grandpa and I picked through everything

in the garage. Here's what we came up with

for the robot: one empty soda can, a broken

remote-controlled car with duct tape, a

transmitter/receiver, four plastic wheels, and a

wire coat hanger.

"Now I have to put these things

together to make my robot," I told Grandpa.

"Not to worry, Sammy-boy. Bet you didn't

know I invented the lightbulb. Never got

credit, because some kid named Edison beat

me to the patent office."

 "I know how to make a robot," Lucy

volunteered. "But I'm not telling."

 "Okay, Lucy. If you're so smart, how do you

do it?"

Lucy picked up a cardboard carton and put it over her head. Then she marched around with stiff arms and legs.

"Very funny," I said. "But this is serious business, so scram!" ONE WAY

Lucy lifted the box off her head. "I'm not leaving. And anyway, Daddy has to come and get me."

I ignored Lucy and got to work on my robot. I took apart the toy car and duct-taped the receiver to the soda can. Grandpa helped me screw on wheels for feet, and we used wire

from the coat hanger for the arms.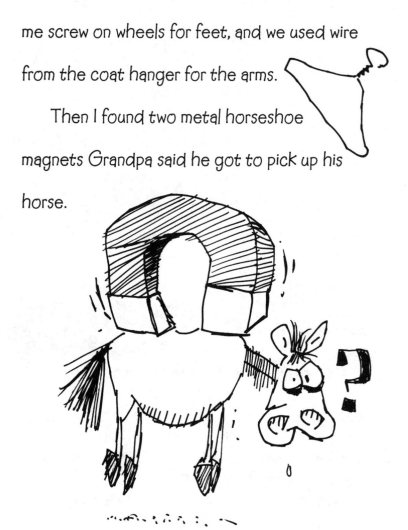

Then I found two metal horseshoe

magnets Grandpa said he got to pick up his

horse.

I attached a magnet to each arm of the

robot for hands.

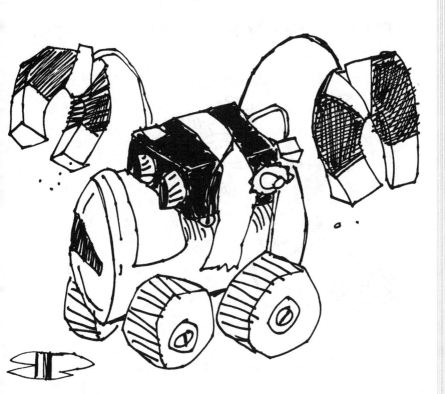

"Now let's see if this robot's going to

work," Grandpa said.

I put the robot down on the garage floor

and pressed the button on the transmitter.

The robot rolled for a bit and then

tumbled over.

"Balance the wheels, Sammy-boy,"

Grandpa said. "That should do it."

I carefully bent the wheels so they faced

forward. "Okay, here goes," I said.

I put the robot back on the ground and

pressed down on the transmitter button. The

robot rolled across the garage without

falling over!

YES!

"I'm proud of you, Sammy-boy," Grandpa

said. "Did it all by yourself, too."

Lucy was staring at the robot. "All it

does is roll around," she said. "An invention's

supposed to do something."

I looked at the robot. Attached to one of the horseshoe magnets was a metal screw!

"It's my 'Metal-Detector Robot,'" I told Lucy. "And it's better than a robot that cleans toilets. This robot can detect land mines buried under your dirty clothes!"

BAMMO

Grandpa and I high-fived. "I'm going to win the Invention Fair!" I yelled.

I helped Grandpa close up the garage, and
Lucy followed us back into the house.

"Mom, look what I invented," I said, holding
up my robot. "It can detect metal things."

"That's wonderful, Sam. But now Lucy has
to get ready to go home. Her dad will be here
soon to pick her up."

"I'll wait outside for my daddy," Lucy said,

putting on her jacket.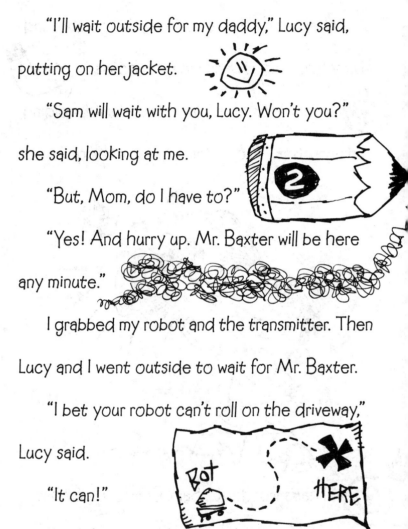

"Sam will wait with you, Lucy. Won't you?"

she said, looking at me.

"But, Mom, do I have to?"

"Yes! And hurry up. Mr. Baxter will be here

any minute."

I grabbed my robot and the transmitter. Then

Lucy and I went outside to wait for Mr. Baxter.

"I bet your robot can't roll on the driveway,"

Lucy said.

"It can!"

I put the robot down on the driveway and

pressed the transmitter button. The robot

started to roll.

"See, I knew it would work!"

"Here comes Daddy," Lucy said. Mr.

Baxter's car started pulling into the driveway.

"Look out for the robot!" I yelled as loud

as I could. But it was too late!

GA-RUNCH!!

Chapter Seven
A Fart-Away Fan Doodle

On Saturday, Cookie came over to my house

to play video games. "Sorry about your robot,

Sam," he said. "Wax is telling everyone you

smashed it on purpose because it didn't work."

"That's not true! It was an accident, and Mr.

Baxter said he was sorry after he ran over it."

"What are you going to do now? The

Invention Fair is next week," Cookie said.

"I'll think of something. Mrs. H. said: All

inventors run into surprises and obstacles along the way."

I plugged in the video game and held my breath. Every time Cookie scores, he farts. He says it's okay to fart, because all NBA players fart in the locker room.

I sniffed the air. Cookie's farts stunk!

Maybe the answer to my invention had been

right under my nose the whole time!

I quickly got up from the couch and shut

off the TV. I had an idea for an invention that

would fix Cookie's problem!

I grabbed a sheet of paper and a pencil,

and doodled a picture of my invention.

"It's a 'Fart-Away Fan,'" I told Cookie,

pointing to my drawing.

"Who needs a Fart-Away Fan?" Cookie

asked. "I don't smell anything."

 "It'll help millions of, um, basketball players."

"How are you going to make that?"

Cookie asked, pointing to my drawing.

 "Easy. I'll buy the mini fan from the

electronics store in the mall. Grandpa can take

us there. And then I can attach the fan to a

hat."

Cookie called his mom. She said he could 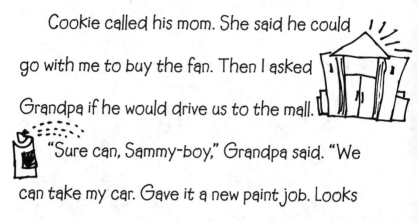 go with me to buy the fan. Then I asked Grandpa if he would drive us to the mall.

"Sure can, Sammy-boy," Grandpa said. "We can take my car. Gave it a new paint job. Looks right pretty now."

Cookie and I hopped into the backseat of Grandpa's car, and we took off for the mall.

When we got there, Grandpa parked the

car, and we went straight to the electronics

store.

The store had shelves full of computers,

cameras, batteries, and video games. I asked

the salesperson where they kept their mini

fans.

"Mini fans are hanging along the back wall,"

she said. Then she asked Grandpa if she could

help him find anything.

"Did I lose something?" Grandpa asked,

checking his pockets.

"Let's go, Grandpa," I said, tugging on his

sleeve. "I have to get the mini fan."

"Look who's over there!" Cookie said as we

walked to the back of the store.  BUY ME!

I turned and saw Robert and New Kid.

They were huddled together near the

cell phone display.

"Hey, Sam, what're you doing here?"

Robert asked when he saw us.

"I'm looking for a mini fan. It's for my new

invention."

"Wax told us what happened to your

robot," New Kid said.

"His dad didn't mean to run it over. It was

an accident. Hey, why are you guys here?"

"Robert's helping me look for a new

phone," New Kid answered. "My dad said I

could buy any one I want."

"Do you want to play b-ball tomorrow?" I

asked Robert.

"I can't. Bradley and I have more work to

do on our invention, then we're playing one-on-

one b-ball."

"But you and I always play one-on-one

b-ball!"

"Maybe next time,"

Robert said.

If we wait until then,

I could be as old as my

grandpa!

That's when I wished Mr. Naismith had

never invented basketball. And that New Kid

had stayed in New York!

Chapter Eight
A Frisbee Doodle

On Monday morning, we gave our oral

reports. Robert went first. He wore a bow tie

and talked funny.

"I'm Sir Alexander Fleming," Robert said.

"I live in Scotland and I invented penicillin. In

World War One, I saw many soldiers die from

infected wounds. After the war, I accidentally

discovered antibiotics, which saved many lives."

New Kid clapped the loudest for Robert.

"Thank you, Robert," Mrs. H. said. "That was very interesting. Now, let's hear from Sam."

I walked to the front of the room and held up a picture of a toilet. "This is my invention," I said. "My name is Thomas Crapper and I'm a plumber. I made toilets better so they wouldn't smell."

"Thomas Crapper didn't invent the toilet!" Wax shouted out. "I read in an invention book that someone else invented an early flush toilet way before Crapper."

"Max, there are several ways to invent," Mrs. H. said. "One way is to invent something original. Another is to make an improvement on something that already exists. That's what Thomas Crapper did."

I shot a look at Wax, but he was busy picking on someone—I mean something—else.

ICK!

The rest of the morning we listened to other kids' reports. Rachel was Ruth Handler, the lady who invented the Barbie doll. Meghan and Nicole were the Wright brothers, but they looked like the Wright sisters!

New Kid was next. He was wearing a white New York Knicks basketball jersey.

"My name is Doctor James Naismith, and I invented basketball," New Kid said. "It was too cold to play outside, so I nailed peach baskets to opposite ends of the gym. Players had to shoot the ball into the basket. I used a soccer ball because basketballs weren't invented yet."

Robert clapped the loudest for New Kid. Then Cookie got up and gave his report. He was Fred Morrison, the guy who invented the Frisbee.

"Good job," Mrs. H. said, after everyone finished giving their reports. "We learned a lot about inventors and their inventions. Now get ready for lunch. The bell is about to ring."

My Fart-Away Fan was tucked inside my backpack. Cookie agreed to eat the chili so we could test it out.

The lunch lady piled chili onto Cookie's

plate, and we carried our trays over to Robert's

table.

New Kid sat down with us. He was still

wearing his white Knicks jersey. "Where'd you

get that jersey?" I asked him. "Is it for real?"

"It used to belong to a famous Knicks

basketball player," he said. "My dad bought

it at an auction. It even has Bill Bradley's

autograph on the back!"

"Wow, that's awesome!" Robert said.

Cookie wolfed down his chili. Now I just

had to wait for him to start farting.

I took the Fart-Away Fan out of my

backpack and turned it on. I felt a breeze as

the blades spun around.

The chili must've gotten to Cookie, because it was the worst fart I ever smelled in my whole entire life! WORST

I put the Fart-Away Fan on my head just as Marvin Willis walked by.

"Hey, Sam, what's up?" he said. Then he made a fist and whacked me on my back.

The Fart-Away Fan flew off the hat and landed in Cookie's plate of chili! But the blades of the fan didn't stop spinning!

1 Whack on back

2 Fan flies off hat

3 Fan lands in chili

4 Chili sprays everywhere

5 including Bradley's DAD's jersey

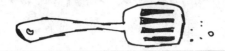

Chapter Nine
A Kitty-Litter Potty
Pooper Doodle

After recess, Wax told Mrs. H. about

chili splattering on New Kid's basketball

jersey. "Now Bradley's going to get in trouble

because his dad didn't know he took it to

school," Wax said.

"It was an accident, Mrs. Hennessey.

Maybe I should've put the fan on better so it

wouldn't have fallen off the hat."

"Sam, you made a prototype. Sometimes

the first working model isn't there yet. But

then you make changes so it works better."

"But, Mrs. Hennessey, it didn't work

the way it was supposed to. We still smelled

Cookie's farts."

"You can improve on your invention or invent something new," Mrs. H. said. "But you don't have much time. The Invention Fair is this Friday."

New Kid didn't talk to me for the rest of the day.

"The fan doesn't work anymore. The chili messed it up," I told Robert. "So now I have to come up with another invention."

"Don't worry," said Robert. "I'm sure you'll come up with something."

Yeah, all by myself!

When I got home from school, Grandpa was in the living room reading the newspaper. Fang, my long-haired rescue cat, was curled up next to him. She has one green eye and one blue eye and her teeth look like fangs. If I entered her in an ugly-cat contest, she'd win first prize.

I walked over and stroked Fang. Then I

sniffed the air. "Something smells good," I told

Grandpa.

"Yup, baked

a batch of catnip

cookies. Fang goes

wild for them.

"And, your mom said to remind you to

clean out Fang's litter box," Grandpa added.

"It stinks just like the time I brought a skunk

into school."

"Why'd you do that,

Grandpa?"

"It was for show-and-

smell, Sammy-boy!"

Scooping Fang's poop is on my "Chore Chart." My mom made up the chart so I can help her do stuff she doesn't like to do.

Here's my "DON'T DO" Chores Chart:

1. Don't clean your room — you're just going to mess it up again.
2. Don't wash dirty underwear — wear it inside out.
3. Don't make your bed — sleep on top of the covers.
4. Don't wash dishes — eat everything on your plate so they _look_ clean.
5. Don't sweep crumbs off the floor — buy a dog instead.

Fang followed me into the bathroom. Her litter box was tucked into a corner next to the toilet. I held my nose and scooped the poop into a plastic bag.

Then I got an idea for a new invention. No one will have to scoop kitty poop ever again!

I grabbed my bottle of Super-Duper Sticky Glue and squirted it all over the toilet seat. After that, I sprinkled on some kitty litter.

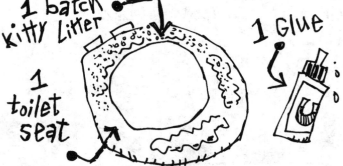

1 batch kitty litter

1 toilet seat

1 glue

"Okay, here's what you do," I instructed Fang. "Sit on this potty seat and poop in the pot."

Fang hopped up onto the edge of the sink and stared at the potty seat. She let out a loud "Meow!" and jumped back down.

I scooped her up and put her back onto the potty seat. But Fang just sat there licking her paws.

After a million minutes, I scrunched up my face and made potty noises to try and get her to poop.

Aargh

plop

TINKLE

Umph

Fang arched her back
and hissed at me. Then she
hopped off the potty seat
and marched straight out
the bathroom door!

Grandpa said he had to use the bathroom,

so I walked back to my bedroom.

Maybe the Kitty-Litter Potty Pooper

wasn't such a great invention after all!

Chapter Ten
A Mad Scientist Doodle

On Wednesday, my mom reminded me that

we had to go to Wax's house for dinner.

"Jeff has a surprise for us," my mom said.

"He'd like us to meet Max and Lucy's aunts,

uncles, and cousins."

"Gee, afraid I can't make it," Grandpa said.

"My favorite show is on TV."

"I can't go, either," I added. "I have to stay

home and look for my stinkbug."

I kept hoping that something would

happen and we wouldn't have to go.

← DOODLES

"Sam, you can ride with Grandpa. I'm taking

my own car, because Jeff and I have plans after

dinner. Grandpa can take you home. And, Sam, I want you to wear your best clothes."

Grandpa was in his bedroom getting dressed. "Hi there, Sammy-boy," he said. "Ready for the big night?"

"I have to go because Mom said so. And I'm bringing Fang because she's part of our family."

"Good idea, Sammy-boy," Grandpa said. "She can wear my bow tie. Fancy her up for the party."

I changed into my good clothes and put

Fang in her carrier. Then Grandpa and I drove

to the Baxter Funeral Home.

Their apartment was above the funeral

home. The good thing was that you could

make all the noise you wanted and the people

downstairs wouldn't complain!

Grandpa and I walked up a flight of stairs.

Fang was hiding in a corner of her carrier. Even she was creeped out!

Inside the living room were vases filled with flowers.

The dining room table was set with candles, and there were a bunch of balloons in the center.

My mom had gotten there before us.

"Whose birthday is it?" I asked her.

"Jeff said it's a surprise," she answered. "So let's wait and see."

Wax's dad rushed over when he saw us. "Welcome! I'm glad you're here!"

Wax and Lucy were standing next to their dad. "I'm hungry, Daddy," Lucy whined. "When are we going to eat?" **GURGLE GURGLE**

"Hey, Dribble," Wax said. "Thought you'd be home coming up with another crazy invention."

"Come with me, Sam," Mr. Baxter said. "I want you to meet Max and Lucy's grandmother."

Grandma Baxter →

Wax's grandmother was sitting on a chair. She had a small brown dog on her lap.

"I'm Sam Dibble," I said, introducing myself.

"Bo-Bo, say hello to the nice boy," Wax's grandmother said to her dog.

Rrrr...rrr...

95

Bo-Bo growled when I reached out to pet

him. I quickly pulled back my hand. I wouldn't be

able to doodle if I was missing a finger!

"Don't be afraid," Wax's grandmother said.

"Bo-Bo's just a little poochy-woochy."

More people came into the room. Wax

said they were his aunts, uncles, and cousins.

"Please take a seat," Wax's dad said.

"We're ready to start."

All the kids had to sit together. I put

Fang's carrier on the floor by my chair. Then I

sat down.

Wax's cousin Trevor was sitting next to

me. He goes to my school, and he's the best

rapper in fifth grade.

"What's up, dude?" Trevor asked me.

"Did you invent something cool to bring to

school?"

"My first invention got squashed, my second one made a mess and broke, and my third one didn't work," I told Trevor. "So now I have to come up with a new one."

"Max's invention didn't work," Lucy offered. "He made shoes to walk on the ceiling, but he fell on his head."

 Wax told Lucy to keep her mouth shut.

Then his dad tapped on a water glass.

"Everyone, I have an important announcement

to make . . ." YAWN

Suddenly, Bo-Bo growled. I looked to see

what he was growling at.

It was Fang! She must've escaped from her

carrier!

"Sam Dibble, I can't believe you brought

Fang to the party," my mom scolded.

Here's what happened next:

A. Bo-Bo leaped out of Wax's grand-mother's arms and took off after Fang.

B. He chased Fang around the dining room.

C. Wax's grandma ran after Bo-Bo.

D. Fang jumped up onto the dining room table.

E. A candle got knocked over.

F. The sprinkler system was set off.

G. Everyone got soaking wet!

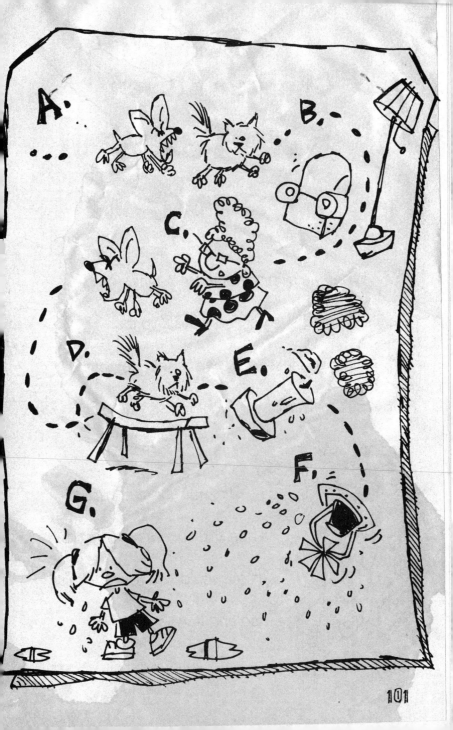

A.

B.

C.

D.

E.

F.

G.

Chapter Eleven
A Stuffed Owl Doodle

When we all got home from Wax's house,

my mom said she wanted to talk to me.

"I know I messed up the toilet seat, but

it wasn't my fault Fang wouldn't sit on it and

poop," I told her.

"It's not about that, Sam."

Then she took a big breath.

"How would you feel if Wax's

dad and I got married?"

"I like things the way they are," I told her.

"And I don't want anything to change."

"Sometimes change can be good," my mom said. "Our family will grow and be even better than before."

But then Wax and I would be brothers!

On Thursday morning in school, Wax said,

"Hey, Dribble, my dad told me he wants to

marry your mom."

If my mom marries Wax's dad, really

bad things could happen:

1. I'd have to call Wax "bro."

2. I'd have to call Lucy "sis."

3. I'd have to call Mr. Baxter "Dad."

At lunch, New Kid told me that his dad got

married, and he had a new little brother. "It's not

so bad, because I go visit them every summer."

"Maybe Wax will move into your house,"

Robert said. "Then you'll have to share all your

things with him!"

My stomach felt
like the time we had
a contest to see who
could eat the most
donuts and I won.

"Or what if you have to move into Wax's

house?" Robert asked.

I'd have to sleep above the dead people!

What if there were ghosts?

After recess, Mrs. H. said that we were going to visit Mr. Howell's fifth-grade class to see some of their inventions. "They made a project using wheels, axles, pulleys, and inclined planes," she said.

Inside Mr. Owl's classroom were shelves filled with bird's nests, seashells, and shiny rocks. There was a microscope and glass slides on each table. The stuffed owl was sitting on his desk.

"Welcome," Mr. Owl said as we filed into the classroom. "Everyone, please take a seat."

After we sat down, Mr. Owl stood in front

START

of the class. "My students were asked to think

of a simple task," he explained. "They had to

invent a machine to do that task in a more

complicated way."

Rachel raised her hand. "I saw that on TV,"

she said. "They had a contest, and the winning

team made an invention that turned on a light."

"There are many contests like that one,"

Mr. Owl said. "They were all inspired by a great

cartoonist." **FiNiSH**

I raised my hand. "That's what I want to be

when I get older," I told Mr. Owl.

"He always gets in trouble for doodling,"

Wax called out.

"Bet you can't doodle as good as he can!"

Cookie shouted.

"That's the way some of our most famous

cartoonists got started," Mr. Owl told Wax.

I looked over at Wax and gave him my

monkey face.

"Okay, class, are you going to show these

guys how to put mustard on a hot dog?" Mr.

Owl asked the fifth graders.

The kids were crouched down on the floor.

"Yes, we're ready!" they yelled back.

"Then let the show begin!"

Here's what happened:

A. One student dropped a marble at the top of a ramp.

B. The marble rolled down the ramp.

C. The marble fell into a train car.

D. The train car moved along the tracks.

E. It hit a cup filled with mustard.

F. Mustard spilled onto a hot dog.

"Yay, we did it!" the kids shouted, jumping up and down.

Most of the kids in my class cheered and clapped their hands.

That's when I came up with my new idea for the Invention Fair!

Eureka!

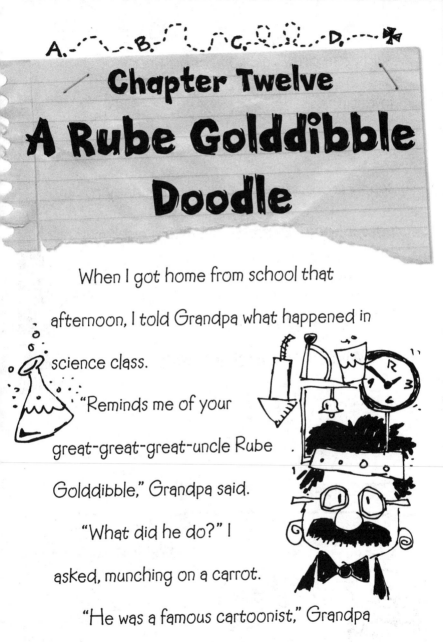

Chapter Twelve
A Rube Golddibble Doodle

When I got home from school that afternoon, I told Grandpa what happened in science class.

"Reminds me of your great-great-great-uncle Rube Golddibble," Grandpa said.

"What did he do?" I asked, munching on a carrot.

"He was a famous cartoonist," Grandpa

said. "He drew cartoons of his wacky

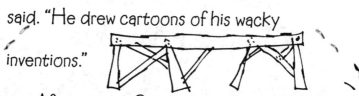

inventions."

After dinner, Grandpa drove me to the art-

supply store. I used my allowance money to buy

poster board, an eraser, and a new black marker.

"Looks like you came up with a new idea,"

Grandpa said, eyeing my supplies.

"Mrs. H. told us that inventors have to

think creatively to solve a problem."

"Yup, one time I had to cook a hot dog,"

Grandpa said. "So I invented fire, Sammy-boy!"

I spent the whole night working on my new idea. Then on Friday morning, I brought it into school.

The Invention Fair was being held in the gym. Mrs. Lewis was standing outside the entrance. "The tables are all marked," she said.

MRS. HENNESSEY
ROOM 210

I walked around until I found our table. Wax was already there. "Hold this for me, Dribble," he said, handing me a small cardboard box.

"What is it?" I asked Wax, turning the box over in my hand.

"It's a 'Super Snot Saver.' My dad said

I should apply for a patent. This invention could earn me millions of dollars!"

"It looks like a plain old box to me, Wax. How does it work?"

"Dribble, don't you know anything? You put snot in the box. Then let's say you don't want

to go somewhere. You take out the snot and tell everyone you're sick and can't go."

Rachel walked over to the table. She was carrying a bowl of spaghetti. "No one

eat this," she warned.

"It's to demonstrate my

'Spaghetti Spin Fork.'"

Meghan and Nicole put their "Baby Buzzer"

on the table.

"It beeps when the baby

cries," Meghan explained.

"My dad helped us make

it," Nicole said.

Then Cookie set up his

model of the "Doggie Bath."

"There's water in the bucket

so the judges can see how it

works," he said.

Next, New Kid and Robert put their "Four-Footed Friend's Ramp" on the table. "We're going to win the grand prize," New Kid declared.

I think Robert should win first prize for worst best friend ever!

Mrs. H. hurried over. "Judging is about to begin," she said. "Does everyone have their inventions?"

"Sam doesn't have one," Wax said. "So he's an automatic loser."

"No, I'm not, Wax!" I said. "My invention is a surprise."

I quickly pointed to my poster board. It was covered with a sheet of paper so no one could see what was underneath.

Mr. Owl was the judge for the Invention Fair. He walked around the gym looking at everyone's invention.

When he got to mine, I whipped off the sheet of paper. "Ta-da!" I said. "Here are the plans for an invention to sharpen your pencil."

"Sharpen a Pencil" Invention:

A. A student releases a mouse from its cage.

B. The mouse runs onto a treadmill.

C. The treadmill turns the handle of a pencil sharpener.

D. The pencil gets sharpened.

E. Sam draws doodles.

Mr. Owl studied my drawing for a long time.

Then he let out a huge laugh!

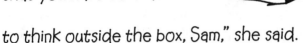

Mrs. H. said she really liked the drawing of my invention. "You showed that you have confidence to think outside the box, Sam," she said.

In the end, a fifth-grade girl won the prize for "Best Overall Invention." Her invention was a "Bitey-Safe Bag" for a bite plate.

Wax won for "Grossest Invention." Robert and New Kid got the "Best Pet Invention" award. The rest of the kids got "Honorable Mention." Even I got a prize!

After the Invention Fair, Wax said I cheated because I didn't make a real invention.

"Did, too," I told Wax. "It's a great way to get your pencil sharpened."

Then New Kid said he wanted me to come over to his house to play b-ball. "You could wear my dad's jersey, Sam," he offered. "It's clean now. Bill Bradley's a really famous player."

"I thought you and Robert were getting together."

"Yeah, but Robert told me you're his best friend. He said that lots of times."

"He did?"

"I have a best friend, too," New Kid said.

"But he goes to my old school."

It would stink if Robert moved away. Then I'd have to find a new best friend.

Robert and I are already thinking about an invention for next year's fair.

And I'm working on a new doodle. But that's another story!

HA!

2B Continued...

About the Author

J. Press has taught millions of kids how to doodle. She majored in doodling at Syracuse University and went on to get a master of doodling at the University of Pittsburgh. At home she enjoys spending time doodling with her children and grandchildren. In her spare time she . . . guess what? You're right! She DOODLES!

About the Illustrator

Michael Kline (Mikey) received a doctorate in applied graphite transference from Fizzywiggle Polytechnic and went on to deface (sorry, *illustrate*) over forty books for children, the most notable being one with J. Press involving an ambulance-chasing peanut. The deadly handsome artist calls Wichita, Kansas, home, where he lives with his very understanding wife, Vickie, felines Baxter and Felix, and two sons.